Layla
the Candyfloss
Fairy

by Daisy Meadows

ORCHARD

www.rainbowmagic.co.uk

The Fairyland Palace

Candy Land

Goblins' ice cream va...

Market ...

Charlie's ice cream

Kirsty's Ho...

Wetherbury Village

Jack Frost's Spell

I have a plan to cause some strife
And use those fairies to change my life.
I'm going to take their charms away
And make my dreams come true today!

I'll build a castle made of sweets,
And spoil the fairies' silly treats.
I just don't care how much they whine,
Their cakes and lollies will be mine!

Contents

Wheeeee!

Kirsty Tate smiled to herself as she
began climbing the steps up the helter-
skelter with her best friend Rachel
Walker. Today she felt like the luckiest
girl in the whole world. Not only was
it her birthday, but she was here at
Wetherbury Park funfair with Rachel,
and the sun was beaming down too.

Best of all, she and Rachel were in the middle of another wonderful magical fairy adventure, this time helping the Sweet Fairies!

"It's a long way up," Rachel commented from behind Kirsty as they went on climbing the steps. "We'll be able to see for miles from the top."

"Yes," Kirsty agreed. Then she lowered her voice. "We might even be able to see a fairy from up there!"

She crossed her fingers hopefully at the thought. Meeting another fairy would make her birthday absolutely perfect!

It was the spring holidays and so far the girls had had a very exciting couple of days. At the start of the week, Honey the Sweet Fairy had surprised them by appearing in a pile of sweets in Kirsty's bedroom. She needed the girls' help to stop Jack Frost, who was up to his naughty tricks again. This time, he'd stolen the Sweet Fairies' magical charms so he could build himself an enormous Candy Castle.

The seven Sweet Fairies worked very hard to make sure that sweets and treats in Fairyland and the human world tasted utterly scrumptious. Without the fairies' magic charms, sweet things didn't taste nice at all. Even worse, it was now the annual Treat Day in Fairyland. The fairy king and queen wouldn't be able to give out their traditional treat baskets to the other fairies, unless all seven charms could be safely returned.

Kirsty and Rachel had been helping the Sweet Fairies track down their magical charms and so far they'd found five: the lollipop, cupcake, ice cream, cocoa bean and cookie charms. Now there were just two fairies missing their magical objects – Layla the Candyfloss Fairy and Nina the Birthday Cake Fairy. And with Kirsty's birthday tea planned for that afternoon, she really hoped they could help both fairies before it was too late!

Just then, she reached the top of the

steps, and let out a
gasp. "Wow!" she
said. "You can see
the whole funfair
from up here!"

Wetherbury Park
was usually a quiet, calm place, with
dog-walkers and joggers, but today it
was full of bustle and noise. It seemed
the whole village had come to the
funfair today.

"There's the teacup ride," Rachel said,
pointing it out. "Oh, and the coconut
shy right next to it."

"I can see my mum and dad!" Kirsty
cried, waving excitedly. "Look, they're
just by the candyfloss stand. I hope that
means we can have one when we meet
them."

"Ooh yes," Rachel agreed. "And there's the mirror maze, I love those," she added. "But I can't see any fairies. Or goblins…"

Kirsty's eyes narrowed as she scanned the crowds of people and the many stalls and attractions below, looking for a telltale flash of green. The goblins were Jack Frost's helpers, and always up to mischief. But like Rachel she couldn't see a single one out there today.

"Ready when you
are," said the
man running
the helter-
skelter.
"Are you
girls riding
together, or
separately?"

"Together," the girls
chorused, then grinned. *Everything* was
more fun when they did it together!

They squeezed onto a long scratchy
mat, Rachel behind Kirsty with her arms
around Kirsty's waist. Then they pushed
themselves off and went whizzing away
down the twisty slide.

"Wheeeee!" cried Rachel happily, her
hair streaming out behind her.

"I feel like I'm flying!" Kirsty laughed, the air rushing past her face.

Rachel blinked as she spotted a tiny glowing object in midair beside them.

She rubbed her eyes and peered closer
– then beamed. "Well, someone here
really *is* flying," she said, pointing out
the sparkling figure at their side. "Look,
Kirsty, it's Layla the Candyfloss Fairy!"

Fluffy Floss

Layla was a very pretty little fairy. She had blonde hair with a fringe and pink-tipped ends, as if it had been dipped in strawberry sauce. She wore a bright pink, flowery dress with a pale pink leather jacket, and matching pink polka-dot shoes. Even her cute ankle socks were pink! "Hello there," she said, fluttering over to land on Kirsty's hand, "and a very happy birthday to you, Kirsty!"

19

"Thank you!" replied Kirsty breathlessly, as they hurtled around another corner. "I'm sure it's going to be an even better birthday now you've come along.

Have you managed to find your magic candyfloss charm yet?"

"No," Layla said, darting into Kirsty's pocket, "but I'm sure it's somewhere at the fair. Would you two mind helping me look for it?"

Neither Rachel nor Kirsty could reply

for a moment as they bumped down the end of the helter-skelter. They staggered to their feet, giggling and feeling rather dizzy.

"That was such fun!" Rachel said. "And of course we'll help you, Layla."

"Thank you," Layla said, her eyes twinkling as she peeped out of Kirsty's pocket. "That *was* fun, wasn't it? Almost as good as flying."

Then her little nose twitched. "Ooh, I smell candyfloss," she said happily. "The best smell in the world!"

"There's my mum and dad," Kirsty said, waving as she spotted them nearby. "And look what they're holding!"

"Candyfloss." Rachel laughed. "Perfect!"

"Hello there," Mrs Tate said, as Kirsty and Rachel went over. "That looked exciting."

"We thought you might like this to share," said Mr Tate, passing Kirsty a huge stick of candyfloss. It was pale pink and glittering with sugar.

"Thank you," Kirsty said, trying not to giggle as she thought about Layla hiding in her jacket pocket. "I was just thinking I'd like some delicious candyfloss. You must have read my mind!"

"We're going to have a cup of tea now," Mrs Tate went on, "so shall we meet you back here in half an hour?"

"Sounds perfect," Rachel replied. "See you later. And thanks for the candyfloss!"

"Yum," Kirsty said, as her parents walked away with a wave. "This looks delicious."

Layla popped her head out and eyed the candyfloss. "It looks great, but remember, it might not taste that way," she said. "Without my magical candyfloss charm, I can't be sure how nice it'll be.

Maybe I should test it first?"

"Okay," Kirsty agreed. "I'll break a bit off for you." She pinched the top of the candyfloss, expecting a piece to pull away easily in her fingers. But instead it felt as hard as rock. "That's strange," she said, pulling harder. "It's really tough."

Layla bit her lip. "That doesn't sound good," she said.

Rachel also tried to snap a clump of candyfloss off, but she couldn't manage it either. "We'll break our teeth on this if we bite into it," she said worriedly.

"And so will anyone else who buys it."

"Oh dear," Layla said, and pointed her
wand at the candyfloss. She murmured
a few magic words and the candyfloss
sparkled all over with
pink and silver
light. Then a
fairy-sized
ball of it
broke away
and flew
through the
air to land in
Layla's hand.
She nibbled at it
carefully and then
screwed up her face in
disgust. "Yuck! It tastes horrible," she
cried. "Jack Frost has ruined it!"

Rachel and Kirsty felt sorry for Layla. She looked so upset. Then Rachel spotted three boys on the teacup ride, who were all tucking into enormous sticks of rainbow-striped candyfloss. They seemed to be eating it perfectly well. "Look! Not all of the candyfloss is ruined," she said, pointing out the boys to Kirsty and Layla. "Maybe the stick your parents bought was just a bad one."

Layla peered thoughtfully at the rainbow candyfloss. "It does look good," she agreed. "Soft, fluffy, delicious. Just the way candyfloss should be. They're certainly enjoying it."

The boys' faces were largely hidden by the huge candyfloss sticks but just then, their teacup spun around and the girls were able to see them more clearly. Rachel, Kirsty and Layla all gasped as they noticed how green the boys' skin was, and what pointy noses they had too.

"Goblins!" they cried.

Chasing Rainbows

Once the three friends had seen the first group of goblins, they began seeing them all over the place. There were goblins at the hoopla stand, tripping over their own big green feet as they clumsily threw the hoops. There were goblins trying and failing to win a big teddy bear at the hook-a-duck game. And there were goblins queuing up for the ghost train, looking a bit nervous at the sounds of screams and yells coming from inside.

What was more, every single one of the goblins was carrying a huge stick of fluffy rainbow-striped candyfloss.

"Where are they getting them all from?" Kirsty wondered aloud.

"Someone is obviously making yummy candyfloss *somewhere*," Rachel replied, glancing around.

"And I bet whoever it is has my candyfloss charm," Layla added. "If we can just get it back, then I could make *all* the candyfloss taste good again." She fluttered out of Kirsty's pocket. "Maybe we'll be able to look around the fair quicker if you two are both fairies. What do you think?"

"Ooh yes, definitely," Kirsty said at

once. She felt giddy with excitement
as she and Rachel ducked behind a
popcorn stand where nobody would see
them. How she loved being a fairy, and
on her birthday, too!

Layla waved her wand and a stream
of pink glittery fairy dust came out in
little puffs. They looked just like tiny
candyfloss clouds, thought Rachel
with a smile as the sparkly dust swirled
around her and Kirsty. Then, in the next
moment, the girls felt
themselves shrinking
smaller and smaller
until they were
fairy-sized too,
with their own
glimmering wings
on their backs.

With just a few flutters they were
sailing up into the air, and neither girl
could help smiling. Being able to fly was
way better than any helter-skelter ride!

"Now then," said Layla, peering down
eagerly at the funfair below. "Eyes
peeled for signs of
anyone making
or selling the
rainbow-
striped
candyfloss."
The three
of them began
searching around the
funfair. There was so much to see, and
so many people that they had to look
very carefully indeed. "Well, there's
the pink candyfloss stand," Kirsty said,

pointing down at it. "That must be where my mum and dad bought the horrible candyfloss for us."

The stall was deserted. "Well, at least nobody's buying anything from there now," Layla said with a little shudder. "I would hate anyone else to be disappointed at how awful it tastes."

But she'd spoken too soon. In the very next moment, the fairies saw a customer walk up to the stand.

"Oh no!" said Rachel. "Do you think we should warn him somehow?"

"We can't let anyone see us," Layla reminded her. "But let's fly closer and see what happens. I might be able to use some fairy dust to make the candyfloss taste a bit nicer."

The three friends fluttered down and

landed on the top of the candyfloss
stand. They could see that the customer
was wearing a bright green clown suit
complete with a curly wig, enormous
shoes and a bright green round nose.

Moments later, the clown walked away
with two big pink candyfloss sticks.

"Oh dear," Kirsty said. "He's in for a
horrible surprise now, poor clown."

Layla raised her wand. "Maybe I can quickly work some magic on that candyfloss," she murmured. "Now, let me see…"

But just before Layla could chant a spell, something very strange happened. The candyfloss began to transform all by itself, from the hard pink candyfloss the clown had bought, into fluffy rainbow-striped candyfloss!

"Wow," Rachel said. "Your magic worked very quickly, Layla. Brilliant!"

Layla looked startled. "I didn't do anything," she said. "Either that clown has magic powers or…"

She stopped speaking and stared at the clown in surprise. He'd just taken an enormous mouthful of the soft, sweet candyfloss. And in doing so, his clown nose had popped off and fallen to the ground! As his real nose appeared, the fairies noticed just how green and pointy it was.

"He's a goblin!" Kirsty gasped.

"Yes, and if he's able to turn bad candyfloss into good, he must have my magic charm," Layla realised. "So *that's* where all the candyfloss is coming from!"

Mirror, Mirror

Just then, the three fairy friends heard excited voices.

"Look, it's a clown!"

"And he's got some of the rainbow candyfloss!"

Rachel, Kirsty and Layla peeped down to see a group of children approaching, all staring at the clown with wide eyes. One of them, a boy in a red T-shirt, stepped forward.

"Excuse me," he said politely, "we were just wondering…"

The clown looked annoyed to be disturbed. "Go away," he snapped. "Can't you see I'm busy?"

"We've been looking everywhere for the rainbow candyfloss," a girl with blonde plaits piped up. "We just wanted to know where you bought yours?"

"Not telling," the clown snapped. "And I'm not sharing either, before you ask. Now, hop it!"

The children looked disappointed. "But we only wanted to know—" the boy tried again, but the clown had turned on his heel and stalked away.

"Wait!" called a girl in a purple top. "Come back, please!"

The children followed the clown, who made an impatient growling sound when he realised.

"Shoo!" he said. "Leave me in peace!"

And he dashed into the nearby mirror maze, clearly hoping to shake them off.

41

"Come on," Layla said quickly as he vanished. "We mustn't let him get away. Let's follow him."

The fairies fluttered into the mirror maze, making sure they flew high up near the ceiling so they wouldn't be noticed. The three children ran after the clown but quickly lost their way in the confusing maze.

"Where *is* he?" the fairies heard one of the boys cry.

"We only wanted to buy some candyfloss!" another girl said. "Why did he run off like that?"

The fairies zipped through the maze until they caught up with the clown who was muttering crossly to himself. "Wretched children!" he complained. "They're as bad as the other goblins, pestering me all the time for more candyfloss. When they know full well that I'm meant to be taking it back for Jack Frost's Candy Castle."

Layla, Kirsty and Rachel froze in midair at the mention of Jack Frost. They all listened hard as the goblin went on moaning to himself.

43

"Wants to use it for candyfloss hedges in the shape of his head, he says. But as fast as I get the candyfloss, it just gets eaten. It'll be tiny candyfloss bushes at this rate, not hedges," he grumbled. "And here's me, slaving away, non-stop! More trouble than it's worth, this magic charm. Just my bad luck to get it!"

"Fancy using my delicious candyfloss to make *hedges*!" Layla hissed, looking very indignant. "Honestly!"

"Well, we know he's definitely got the charm now, at least," Rachel whispered. "So all we have to do is get it back."

44

"Maybe we could—" Kirsty began, but then broke off as they all heard the children approaching once more.

"He must have gone *this* way," a boy was saying.

"Come on, we've got to find him," a girl added. "He can't be far away."

Hearing the children's voices, a look of panic appeared on the clown's face. "Oh, great," he grumbled, rushing forward. Unfortunately he ran straight into a mirror. He had reached a dead end!

"Oh, *no*!" he moaned, as the voices grew louder. Any moment now, the children would track him down, and he would be trapped!

Rachel had an idea and bravely flew down in front of the clown's face. "Hi," she said cheerfully. "I've got a suggestion to make."

The clown jumped when he saw Rachel, and all her fairy reflections.

"Go away!" he hissed, trying to bat her with his sticks of candyfloss. "Children… Fairies… Why can't you all just buzz off?"

"I can help you," Rachel insisted, darting out of reach. "We can all help you."

Kirsty and Layla flew down then, dancing lightly through the air in front of him.

The clown looked thoroughly fed-up.

"Why did I ever come into this stupid maze?" he complained.

"I've no idea why *you* came in here, but I can tell you why *we* did," Layla retorted, quick as a flash. "To get my candyfloss charm back!"

47

"Never," the clown snarled. "It's mine now, Jack Frost said so."

"Ahh, but what if we could help you get away from the children?" Rachel said. "Would you give it to us then?"

"We could make a deal," Kirsty added quickly. "You said yourself that having the charm is too much hard work, after all."

"Surely you don't want to be trapped by all those noisy children…" Layla coaxed, as their voices grew louder still.

Then Kirsty saw the boy in the red
T-shirt appear a few metres away.
"There he is!" he cried. "I've found
him!"

Boing!

The clown gulped as he saw all the children charging towards him.

"Oh, all right, all right," he muttered to the fairies. "You can have the stupid charm. Just don't let them catch me and take all my candyfloss!"

Layla waved her wand and zipped into action immediately. With a bright flurry of pink sparkles, a new mirror appeared, slicing through the short corridor between the children and the clown.

"Whoa, that was weird," the girls and Layla heard the boy say to his friends. "I'm *sure* he was there a minute ago. It was as if he just magically disappeared!"

The clown chortled. "Nice work, fairy," he said.

But Layla hadn't finished. Two seconds later, one of the mirrors behind the clown vanished, giving him an easy escape route through the maze. "There," she said. "How's that?"

"Wow," the clown marvelled, his eyes boggling at

her amazing magic. "Cheers for that."
And in the next moment, he'd turned
and dashed away, his long clown shoes
slapping against the floor.

"Wait a minute," Layla called, flying
after him. "Don't forget the deal. You
have to give me my charm back now."

"No chance," he yelled over his
shoulder. "So long, losers!"

"Hey!" Rachel cried. "That's not fair. You agreed, fair and square!"

The clown just laughed and kept running. He ran all the way out of the maze and through the funfair, still clutching the candyfloss. Kirsty, Rachel and Layla flew as fast as they could behind him, but couldn't quite catch up.

"We can't let him get away," Layla said. "Keep flying, girls!"

The clown ran out of the funfair and into a small copse of trees at the edge of the park. The fairies flew after him into a clearing, where they saw a huge mound of rainbow-coloured candyfloss.

"Wow," Rachel said, staring in surprise. "It's like a candyfloss mountain."

The clown turned round, hearing her words. "Yes, and you're not having any of it," he told the fairies sharply. "I've worked my socks off, collecting this lot for Jack Frost's hedges. Best candyfloss in town, this is." He pulled a face at Layla. "I think you should let me keep your candyfloss charm, actually," he went on. "I reckon I'm much better at making this stuff than any fairy."

"Oh, really?" said Layla crossly.

"Yeah, really," he retorted, climbing
up the colourful mountain
to dump his new
candyfloss on top.
"Look at this," he
said, bouncing
on his toes, and
springing back
up from the
fluffy floss.
"Super-soft and
super-bouncy.
Perfect!"

Layla was about to argue with him,
but just then Kirsty had an idea and
quickly spoke first. "That *does* look
bouncy," she said admiringly. "I bet it
makes a brilliant trampoline. Can I have
a go on it?"

"Oh yes, me too!" Rachel cried. "Please?"

The clown sneered down at them. "No way," he told them. "This is my candyfloss mountain, and if anyone's going to bounce on it, it's me. Watch this!"

He gave an enormous leap on the top of the mountain before boinging straight back up again. "Ha ha!" he chortled. "This is *fuuuun!*"

Layla sighed. "I can't bear to watch," she said. "He's ruining the only nice candyfloss in the whole fair with those huge dirty feet of his."

"Wait," Kirsty urged in a low voice. "I'm hoping all the bouncing might shake the candyfloss charm loose if it's in his pocket. You never know."

"Good idea." Layla smiled. "Let's hope so."

But unfortunately the magical charm didn't fly out of the clown's pocket – because just then his big clown shoes made him stumble. "Whoa!" he yelled as he toppled over and went rolling down the mountain. "Help!"

Rachel, Kirsty and Layla couldn't help giggling as he rolled down. Strands of sticky candyfloss wound around him as he went and by the time he'd reached the bottom he was at the middle of a tightly wrapped candyfloss ball, with his head sticking out of one end, and his clown feet out the other!

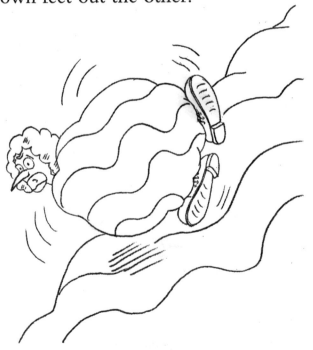

Layla grinned. "Whoops," she said to the clown. "How on earth are you going to get out of *that*?"

Candyfloss Capture!

"Help!" the clown called, thrashing
his head around as he struggled to free
himself. It was no use, though. He was
completely stuck in the ball of candyfloss
and merely rolled a little from side to
side, like a beetle on its back.

"Help?"
echoed Rachel,
pretending to
think. "But
last time we
helped you,
you broke
our deal. Why
would we want
to help you again?"

"It's true," Layla said.
"If you'd given me the candyfloss charm
the first time, we might be willing to help
you out of there now, but…"

She deliberately left the sentence
hanging and the clown let out a groan.

"Oh, all right," he grumbled. "If I give
you the charm, will you help me out of
this candyfloss ball?"

Kirsty grinned. "We will," she said. "But this time, you give us the charm first."

The clown heaved a sigh. "It's in my shoe," he muttered. "Help yourself."

Layla quickly turned Kirsty and Rachel back into girls and they ran around the candyfloss ball to the goblin's feet. They each pulled off one of his huge shoes and cheered as a pink candyfloss-shaped charm on a silver necklace fell to the ground with a tinkling sound.

"Hooray!" cried Layla,
swooping down
towards it. As soon
as she touched
the charm,
it shrank
down to
fairy-size
and she
fastened it
gratefully around
her neck. There was a sudden flash
of bright pink light and the little fairy
gave a big smile. "My candyfloss magic
is working properly again," she said
happily. "Now all the candyfloss should
be yummy everywhere once more. And
those children at the fair will be able to
enjoy a tasty treat!"

"Yay!" Rachel smiled. "Well done, Layla."

"And well done, you two as well!" she replied. "I couldn't have done it without your help, that's for sure."

A grumpy cough came from the clown. "Ahem," he said. "Aren't you lot forgetting something? Our deal?"

Layla's eyes sparkled mischievously. "A fairy never breaks a promise," she said. "Unlike *some* people I could mention…" She waved her wand and magic sparkles puffed out of it.

As soon as the fairy magic touched the huge candyfloss ball, it began to dissolve, twirling up into the air like smoke. After a few moments, the clown was free, and there was just a single clump of candyfloss left, perfectly forming the shape of Jack Frost's head.

The clown looked unhappy when he saw it but muttered his thanks and plodded off. "I hope he won't be *too* cross with me," the girls heard him saying as he went away clutching the candyfloss.

"Thanks again," Layla said spinning happily in midair. "I'd better get back to Fairyland now, to make some special candyfloss for the Treat Day baskets. If I hurry, I'll just be in time. But before I go, you'd better have these."

She waved her wand and two big sticks of fluffy rainbow candyfloss appeared in Kirsty and Rachel's hands. "Goodbye!"

"Goodbye!" called Kirsty and Rachel. "And thank you!" They waved as Layla zipped away, a tiny speck of glowing light against the blue sky.

"We'd better go and meet my mum and dad now," Kirsty said, noticing the time. She took a bite of her candyfloss as they walked. "Oooh! That is so fluffy. And lovely and gooey in your mouth."

"Yum," said Rachel, enjoying a mouthful of hers too. "The nicest candyfloss I've ever had. And look how sparkly it is. Definitely a fairy magic special."

"Helping Layla was really fun," Kirsty said happily as they made their way back through the fairground.

"And now there's only one Sweet Fairy left to help."

Rachel grinned. "Nina the Birthday Cake Fairy," she remembered. "We've *got* to help her get her magical charm back, Kirsty, so that all birthday cakes taste yummy, including yours!"

"You're right," said Kirsty. "But whatever happens, so far this has definitely been my most exciting birthday ever!"

Now it's time for Kirsty and
Rachel to help...

Nina the Birthday Cake Fairy

Read on for a sneak peek...

"What an amazing birthday this has
been!" said Kirsty Tate, doing a twirl in
the middle of the pavement.

"It's been the best birthday ever,"
agreed her best friend Rachel Walker.
"I've enjoyed it just as much as you,
even though it's not MY birthday!"

Rachel was visiting the Tate family
for the spring half term, and they were
all walking home with Kirsty's parents
from Wetherbury Park, where they had
been celebrating Kirsty's birthday at the
village funfair.

"So what's been the best thing about

your birthday?" asked Mr Tate.

Kirsty threw her hands into the air.

"I can't decide!" she said with a laugh. "Everything has been perfect. Rachel's here for a visit, Aunt Harri gave us a guided tour of *Candy Land*, and we've had a brilliant time at the funfair."

"Well, your birthday is about to get even better," said Mrs Tate.

Kirsty stopped and looked at her parents and her best friend. Their eyes were sparkling with happiness.

"We've all got another birthday surprise for you," Mr Tate added.

Kirsty looked at their smiling faces in excitement.

"You have to tell me what the surprise is!" she pleaded.

Rachel shook her head.

"That would spoil it," she said. "Come on, let's hurry back home."

The girls held hands and rushed ahead.

"It's really hard to keep secrets from you," Rachel said in a breathless voice. "We usually share all our secrets, don't we?"

The girls shared one of the biggest secrets imaginable. They were friends of Fairyland, and their latest magical adventures were some of the most thrilling they had ever had.

Read Nina the Birthday Cake Fairy to find out what adventures are in store for Kirsty and Rachel!

Meet the
Sweet Fairies

**If Kirsty and Rachel don't find
the Sweet Fairies' magical charms,
Jack Frost will ruin all sweet treats for ever!**

www.rainbowmagicbooks.co.uk

Meet the fairies, play games
and get sneak peeks at
the latest books!

www.rainbowmagicbooks.co.uk

There's fairy fun for everyone on
our wonderful website.
You'll find great activities, competitions, stories and
fairy profiles, and also a special newsletter.

Get 30% off all Rainbow Magic books at

www.rainbowmagicbooks.co.uk

Enter the code RAINBOW at the checkout.
Offer ends 31 December 2013.

Offer valid in United Kingdom and Republic of Ireland only.

Competition!

The Sweet Fairies have created a special competition just for you!
In the back of each book in the Sweet Fairies series there will
be a question for you to answer. First you need to collect the
answer from the back of each book in the series.
Once you have all the answers, take the first letter from each one
and arrange them to spell a secret word!
When you have the answer, go online and enter!

We will put all the correct entries into a draw and select a winner
to receive a special Rainbow Magic Goodie Bag featuring lots of
treats for you and your fairy friends. You'll also star in a new
Rainbow Magic story!

Who writes the Rainbow Magic books?

Daisy
Meadows

Enter online now at www.rainbowmagicbooks.co.uk

Nicki the Holiday Camp Fairy

Rachel and Kirsty have been looking forward to camp, but everything is going wrong. Can they help Nicki fix things, before the whole summer is ruined?

www.rainbowmagicbooks.co.uk